When 10-year-old Ben Tennyson stumbles upon a mysterious alien device in the woods one summer, little does he realise that his life is set to change - forever.

As soon as the watch-like Omnitrix quite literally gets a grip on him, Ben discovers it gives him the ability to transform into 10 different alien super-beings, each one with awesome powers!

Using the Omnitrix to cause super-powered mischief turns out to be fun, but will Ben learn to use his might to fight for good?

READ ON AND FIND OUT . . .

EGMONT

We bring stories to life

Published in Great Britain 2009
by Egmont UK Limited
239 Kensington High Street, London W8 6SA

Adapted from the animated series by
Barry Hutchison

1 3 5 7 9 10 8 6 4 2

A CIP catalogue record for this title is available from
the British Library

Printed and bound in Great Britain by the CPI Group

BEN 10™
THE GALACTIC ENFORCERS

CHAPTER ONE

A DAY AT THE MUSEUM

Hundreds of light years away, beyond the edges of our galaxy, a swirling yellow wormhole tore open in space. Silently, a small mining ship floated through it. The vessel glided gracefully through a field of asteroids,

before coming to land on the upper deck of a vast space station.

BOOOOM! A powerful energy blast turned the ship to dust. A second ship – this one armed for war – swooped down towards the space station. As it arced past, a bulky shape shot from within.

The object smashed through the upper deck of the station, sending chunks of metal floating off into the vast reaches of space. Inside, it crashed through three more floors, before finally coming to a stop in a wide, dimly lit corridor.

After a moment, the bulky shape slowly stood up, revealing itself to be a huge, dinosaur-headed alien. He stretched his muscular limbs and creaked his thick neck. That landing had been rough, but he'd had worse.

An electrical blast hit him on the chest as the station's automated security systems launched a counter-attack. It gave him a pleasant tickling feeling, but he didn't have time to enjoy it – his name was Vulkanus, and he had a job to do.

A single punch from his spiked fists reduced the security drones to a pile of high-tech junk. His other hand sliced through a thick, metal door like a knife through butter. Ducking his head, he stepped through the broken doorway and into the room beyond.

It was lit only by a faint pink glow, which was coming from a tall glass canister, a small test tube suspended in the air inside it.

Within the test tube, a chunk of strange liquid metal squirmed. Vulkanus allowed himself a toothy grin. He'd found it. He'd found the Element X!

A few minutes later, Vulkanus stepped on to the command deck of his own ship. The captain's chair swivelled round to face him. An alien bounty hunter named SixSix leaned forwards from the shadows.

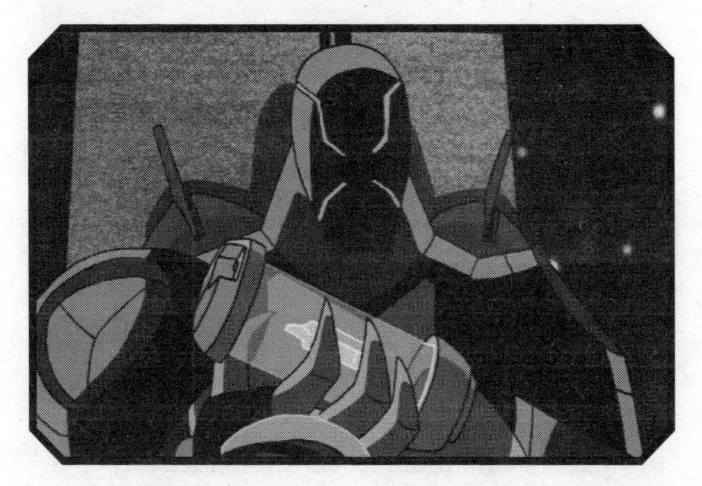

'Element X,' Vulkanus grunted. SixSix held out a slender, gloved hand. 'It's no good by itself, you know,' Vulkanus continued. 'Where are we going to find the bisynthium we need to make it go boom?'

SixSix touched a hidden button on his alien armour. A hologram of a blue-and-green planet suddenly filled the room.

Vulkanus spat in disgust. 'I should have

known. The cesspool of the galaxy.' He scowled. 'Earth!'

* * *

Somewhere else completely, a very different threat was stomping along a crowded street, sending terrified citizens fleeing for safety. A gigantic robot towered above the panicked pedestrians, crushing cars beneath its giant metal feet.

Inside the robot's head, a pudgy little man in a ridiculous tight-fitting costume bounced excitedly in his seat.

'Tremble, insects!' he cried. 'Bow and kiss the feet of Lord Doomicus!'

'Oh, yeah?' called a voice from outside.

Doomicus peered down at the street. An all-too-familiar figure stood atop the wreckage of a car, his cape fluttering in the breeze.

'Ultra Ben!' gasped the villain.

Faster than the eye can see, Ultra Ben flew at the robot, his super-strength muscles tensed and ready. The deafening screech of tearing metal filled the air for a moment before Doomicus's robot toppled to the ground, its legs no longer attached.

'My destructoid!' wailed Doomicus. 'Noooo!'

Standing on the remains of one of the robot's feet, Ultra Ben addressed the grateful crowd that had already begun to form around him.

'And any other chump who makes trouble in Tennyson Town is gonna get the same two-fisted justice!' he announced.

The crowd erupted into whoops and cheers. They punched the air as they chanted his name: 'Ultra Ben! Ultra Ben! Ben! Ben!'

'Ben!' cried another voice. Ultra Ben listened carefully. He recognised the voice, but where from?

'Ben!' shouted Gwen, snapping her cousin out of his daydream. Perched high on a statue of a giant foot, Ben closed his comic book. Wow, those stories could really suck you in!

'That's a work of art, you know,' Gwen snapped, pointing to the statue he sat on. 'Not your personal butt-rest. You're going to get us kicked out of the museum.'

Ben sighed. If only. 'I don't have that kind

of luck,' he said with a shrug.

'One afternoon of culture won't kill you.'

'Unless it bores me to death,' Ben muttered in reply. He rummaged in his pocket and pulled out a square of chocolate.

'Hey, can I have a piece of that?' asked Gwen.

'Sorry,' said Ben with a smirk, hopping down from the statue. 'Chocolate's for superheroes only.'

'More like super-*jerks*,' said Gwen, walking away in a sulk.

Ben shrugged and headed in the opposite direction. He went out on to the museum steps, hoping the fresh air might help keep him awake.

A shadow passed across him. He looked up to see a battle-ready spaceship drift overhead. Its boosters hissed as it came down for a landing in the middle of the road.

'Maybe this won't be such a boring day

after all,' muttered Ben.

A ring of bystanders had gathered around the ship. They chattered excitedly, amazed by what they were witnessing.

All talking stopped as a door in the ship began to slide open. The onlookers held their breath, waiting to see what would emerge from within the alien craft.

Vulkanus strode down the metal walkway and stared at the humans. He sneered in disgust. How he hated these pathetic creatures.

'Take me to your bisynthium alloy,' he demanded in a voice like thunder. The watching people exchanged puzzled glances. He wanted them to take him to the *what*?

The alien scowled. He was wasting his time. These idiots knew nothing. He would just have to find the stuff himself.

Roaring, he slammed a fist against the ground. The shockwave split the concrete into a web-like pattern of cracks, and sent the humans running for their lives.

Ben ducked behind a building and cranked the dial on the Omnitrix.

'Now that's just plain rude,' he mumbled. 'Someone's got to teach Ugly there some manners!'

At that precise moment, 'Ugly' was raining destruction down on the street. He heaved a car up with one hand, and took aim. The vehicle exploded as it smashed into a second-storey window, showering glass on all those below.

The alien paused when something heavy landed on his back. He craned his neck round

to find a figure with red skin clinging to his shoulders.

'OK, tough guy –' began Four Arms.

'A Tetramand?' Vulkanus growled. 'This planet really *is* a dump.'

With a simple shrug, he launched Four Arms backwards through a shop window, and turned his attention back to the business of destroying everything in sight.

But Four Arms wasn't done yet. Roaring, he burst from within the shop, hitting Vulkanus with an explosive right hook. Caught off guard, the evil alien smashed head first through the wreckage of a car. He lay there, dazed and groaning.

A whirring from the spaceship made Four Arms look up. SixSix erupted through a hatch on the ship's roof, his rocket pack shooting him into the air on twin jets of flame.

Four Arms recognised the alien right away. He'd been one of a pack of bounty hunters who had attacked Ben and his family a few weeks ago. He must have escaped from the space prison he'd been slung into.

SixSix cut loose with a hailstorm of laser gunfire. Four Arms dodged the blasts, then launched himself at his enemy, knocking him from the sky. He caught the villain by his armour and hoisted him high off the ground. That had been almost too easy.

Suddenly, something at his feet began to go **TICK TICK TICK**. Four Arms looked down just as a miniature energy bomb exploded. A crackling surge of electricity curved up from the weapon, cocooning his alien body completely. Four Arms roared and struggled against the powerful bonds, but it was no use. No matter how hard he fought, he couldn't escape them!

CHAPTER TWO

THE GALACTIC ENFORCERS

As Four Arms fought against the agonising energy that wrapped round his body, SixSix took aim with his rockets. He was going to turn this meddling fool into a greasy spot on the pavement.

The bounty hunter tried to launch his weapons, but found himself unable to move. A glowing energy field surrounded his body. It held him motionless for a few seconds, before he found himself hurled through the air. As SixSix bounced on the hard ground, the energy field faded away.

The energy snares around Four Arms vanished with a **FZZZT**. Grateful, but a little puzzled, the alien superhero glanced around to see who had saved him from certain doom.

Three bizarre alien figures stood nearby, dressed in matching yellow uniforms. The alien in the middle – a blue-skinned man with a bald head – stepped forwards, his cape billowing in the breeze.

'No *way*!' grinned Four Arms, realising he had just been saved by some real live alien superheroes!

'OK,' said Gwen as she and Grandpa stepped out from the corner where they'd been

hiding. 'This is weird.'

'Rescue formation Alpha Nine!' boomed the bald blue alien.

Finally freeing himself from the wreckage of the car, Vulkanus glared over at the newcomers and spat. 'It's the Capes,' he spat. 'I *hate* Capes.'

The dino-alien dragged SixSix back to his feet, and together they began attacking with everything they had.

The bald-headed alien leaped into the air, avoiding a spray of laser fire from the bounty hunter. Spinning through the sky, he unleashed a powerful blast of heat vision at SixSix's weapon. The gun quickly turned a blistering shade of red before melting away completely.

The second alien superhero ran forwards. This one looked like Four Arms – a *female* Four Arms! She was the red-skinned alien's exact double, aside from her long black hair and skirt.

Slamming all four of her hands together, she sent a shockwave rippling outwards. The wave caught SixSix, lifted him off the ground, then dumped him back down on his head several metres away.

Four Arms shrank back in horror as his female mirror image turned and winked two of her four eyes at him. A love-struck alien heroine really wasn't a problem Ben needed right now!

A short distance away, the strangest of all the aliens was taking care of Vulkanus. This alien looked for all the world like a floating octopus, except where its head should have been, a giant brain pulsed inside a glass jar. On the surface of the glass, a computer-generated face pulled itself into a scowl as Vulkanus attacked.

Gliding upwards, the floating brain easily avoided the dino-alien's punches. Using its special powers, it wrapped Vulkanus in another blue energy field before launching him quickly upwards.

As Vulkanus soared into the sky, the bald-headed alien swooped down and delivered him a knockout punch. Vulkanus dropped like a stone back to Earth, landing on top of SixSix with a nasty crunch.

The flying alien gently drifted down until he hovered above the dazed villains. 'By the provisions set forth in The Galactic Code of Conduct,' he announced, 'I order you to surrender. Will you yield?'

'Yield?' Four Arms frowned. 'What is this, a traffic light? Kick their butts before they try to pull something!'

Too late! A compartment in SixSix's chest flipped open, letting a blinking gadget roll free. It exploded in a dazzling flash of white light, blinding the superheroes.

By the time they were able to see, SixSix and Vulkanus were back in their ship. Four Arms braced himself, ready to leap after the fleeing villains.

Before he could make his move, two short laser blasts zapped from the ship's weapon systems. They tore through the twin stone columns of a nearby building. Without the pillars to support it, the entire building began to topple.

Moving quickly, Four Arms ran through the dust and smoke. His mighty muscles bulged as he caught the front of the building and began to push it back up into position.

He felt his arms and legs begin to shake under the strain. They had to go and pick the biggest, heaviest building to knock over, didn't they? Bad guys could be *so* inconsiderate.

The female four-armed alien appeared at his side. She caught hold of the shattered remains of one of the pillars and heaved. Working together, they managed to push the stone columns back up into place.

'You may release your grip now,' said the octopus-like alien, his brain glowing as he spoke. Focusing hard, he held the vast weight in place with the power of his mind long enough for his friend to melt the stone back together with a blast of her heat vision.

Four Arms suddenly felt a strong grip wrap round his neck. The female alien looked him up and down and smiled.

'So,' she breathed, 'what's a big strong alien like you doing on a planet like this?' She leaned in and fluttered all four sets of eyelashes. 'We make a good team, don't we?'

With a **BLEEP**, the Omnitrix began to flash red. Four Arms broke out into a wide grin of relief. '*Yes!*' he cried. 'Saved by the beep!'

One quick transformation later, Ben stood in the alien's place. The female Four Arms frowned at him, puzzled.

'Hey,' she demanded, 'where'd the rest of you go?'

'Sorry, I'm just a kid,' Ben explained, holding up the Omnitrix for her to see. 'I just get some extra hands once in a while.'

'So it is true,' muttered the floating brain, approaching from above. 'The Omnitrix is in the possession of a child. We had heard you were of

a somewhat limited mental capacity.' The alien noticed Ben's expression. 'No offence,' it added quickly.

Gwen and Grandpa hurried over to join the group. 'Don't worry,' said Gwen, smiling. 'He gets that all the time.'

They all turned as the blue-skinned alien came in to land.

'Greetings,' he beamed, 'I am Ultimos, the Specimen Prime. This is Synaptak and Tini,' he continued, pointing towards the floating brain and the female alien in turn. All three of them suddenly struck a dramatic pose. 'We are – The Galactic Enforcers!' announced Ultimos, in a voice that boomed like thunder.

'Whoa! The uniforms, the moves . . . You guys rock!' chattered Ben. 'Finally, some other superheroes I can hang with!'

'As per The Galactic Code of Conduct, we hereby officially request clearance to operate in your quadrant,' said Ultimos.

Ben glanced up at Grandpa, who could only shrug. 'Uh . . . sure,' Ben replied.

Ultimos nodded once. 'Then we have much to discuss,' he said.

Swishing back his cape, the Specimen Prime touched a button on his Galactic Enforcers badge. Three glowing discs of light appeared beneath Ben, Gwen and Grandpa Max.

The light crept upwards until it covered their entire bodies. Ben grinned as he was suddenly launched upwards at an unbelievable rate.

'All *right*!' he cried.

A few hundred kilometres above the surface of the Earth, the sparkling silver headquarters of The Galactic Enforcers drifted silently through space.

On board, three bright lights signalled the arrival of Grandpa, Gwen and Ben. They paused for a moment, waiting for their stomachs to catch up with them. That had been quite a ride!

Grandpa took a deep breath. 'I never did like those transporter discs,' he muttered.

They turned to find Ultimos, Synaptak and Tini standing behind them. The superheroes gestured for them to take a look around.

'How cool is this?' cried Ben as he took it

all in. A large table in the shape of The Galactic Enforcers' logo filled most of the room. On the walls, spare costumes, weapons and high-tech gadgets were suspended by anti-gravity fields. 'I'm in superhero heaven!' he said, beaming.

'Close your mouth, super-dweeb,' said Gwen with a scowl. 'You're drooling all over the place!'

Grandpa, as usual, was straight down to business. 'So,' he asked, 'why did we have the pleasure of Mr Gadget Guy's company again?'

A holographic projection of the alien bounty hunter suddenly appeared beside Ultimos. 'His name is SixSix,' the enforcer explained. 'He escaped incarceration and formed an alliance with the cretin Vulkanus.'

'A Detrabyte,' added Synaptak, bringing up an image of the dino-headed alien. 'Limited mental capabilities. All brawn, no brains.' He looked at Ben. 'You know the type.'

The hologram shimmered. When it took

form again, it showed an image of the test tube Vulkanus had stolen from the space station.

'They were hired to steal Element X,' Ultimos continued.

The Tennysons exchanged puzzled glances. 'OK, we give up.' Ben shrugged. 'What's Element X?'

The hologram changed yet again. This time it showed a complicated-looking model of Element X's chemical structure. A model of another chemical structure – similar, but not quite the same – hung in the air next to it.

'Element X can be used to form one half of a devastatingly explosive compound,' said Synaptak.

'So, why come to Earth?' asked Ben.

'Most likely in search of the other ingredient,' replied Ultimos. 'Bisynthium alloy. It's very rare, but rumoured to be found on your planet. When combined, the alloy and Element X form an explosive powerful enough to destroy an entire solar system.'

Gwen stared at the hologram. She'd never seen the chemical-structure model of Element X before, but there was something about the second one . . .

'Why does this stuff look so familiar?' She frowned.

'Ah, Gwen,' began Ben, 'I think the giant floating brain guy has it covered.'

'Well, I guess we should get back down there and start looking for them,' said Grandpa Max.

'Excuse me, but The Galactic Code is very clear on our protocol,' announced Ultimos. 'Tini,' he boomed, 'launch Observos one through four!'

Tini crossed to a control panel and pressed a row of buttons. Four miniature satellites launched from below the spacecraft and zipped off towards the distant Earth.

'The Observos will scan every inch of the city and locate the perpetrators,' Ultimos explained. He stepped aside, revealing a shiny metal door. 'In the meantime, perhaps a tour would be in order?'

Max nodded. 'We'd be honoured.'

'Oh, I'm sorry,' said Ultimos, 'but The Galactic Code is quite clear. Provision three seven three dash eight three seven: "No civilian visitors in secure areas of the ship."' He smiled apologetically. 'You and your granddaughter must remain here on the bridge.'

The big blue alien turned to Ben. 'Tini will show you around.'

The female Tetramand yanked Ben off his feet and hoisted him on to her shoulder.

'Hey! How come he gets to go?' demanded Gwen.

Ultimos looked shocked by the question. 'Wearing the Omnitrix grants him *full superhero status*,' he replied. Ben's eyes lit up. Full superhero status. He liked the sound of that!

Synaptak looked on as Tini carried Ben away. For a moment, his digital face seemed to twist into a scowl before he and Ultimos followed Tini off the bridge.

'Don't worry about us. We'll be fine!' Gwen called after them. When they were safely out of earshot, she added: 'Super-jerks,' under her breath.

Ben stared out through a huge bay window at the vastness of space. Stars winked back at him, brighter than any he'd ever seen before. In the distance, the planet Mars slowly spun – a fat, red football orbiting the sun.

'*Whoa!*' Ben whispered. 'That's cool!'

'Ben, here,' Ultimos boomed as he strode into the room to join the boy and his four-armed tour guide. 'I want to show you something.'

The alien superhero stopped at a small table, which had risen from the floor at the sound of his voice. Ben jumped as an enormous hardback book landed on it with a **THWACK!**

'This is The Galactic Code of Conduct,'

Ultimos continued. 'Every Galactic Enforcer must learn the rules, so that they may *live* the rules.'

Ben pulled a face. 'Oh, man! Superhero homework?'

'Well, the first twelve thousand pages are a bit dry,' Ultimos admitted, 'but after that –'

A piercing alarm screeched from hidden speakers, halting the superhero mid-sentence. He squared his jaw and clenched his fists. 'The Observos have discovered something!'

By the time the superheroes made it back to the bridge, Gwen and Grandpa were already studying a video screen. It showed a rough, rocky terrain. Diggers and other heavy machinery littered the landscape.

Suddenly, two familiar figures appeared from behind a truck. SixSix and Vulkanus skulked towards a mound of rock, unaware their every move was being watched.

'That's a strip mine,' said Grandpa. 'Looks like they're after iron ore. Is that the missing ingredient?'

'We'd better get down there,' said Ultimos, frowning. 'But we could use some help.' He turned to Ben and rested a hand on the boy's shoulder. 'Ben, would you consider a temporary commission in The Galactic Enforcers?'

'Good idea!' Tini grinned.

'*Bad* idea!' Synaptak scowled.

'It seems I am the deciding vote,' said Ultimos. He looked down into Ben's hopeful gaze and quickly made up his mind. 'Let's get you in uniform.'

A few short minutes later, the doors to a well-equipped dressing room swished open. A familiar boy in an unfamiliar, oversized costume leaped out, flexing his non-existent muscles.

'Presenting Ultra Ben!' he cried. 'Galactic Enforce–'

Before he could finish, his foot caught on

his cape. Watched by the assembled Galactic Enforcers and his own family, he tripped and landed in an awkward heap.

'I meant to do that,' he groaned.

Grandpa Max turned to Ultimos. 'What about us?' he asked.

'I'm afraid The G.C.C. is quite clear about the participation of non-super-powered beings,' the enforcer replied. 'You'll be safer here.'

Before they could object, an invisible mental shove from Synaptak sent Gwen and Max stumbling back from the transporter.

'Hey!' Gwen snapped. She looked across to her cousin for back-up.

'Sorry, guys.' Ben shrugged, taking a square of chocolate from his pocket and popping it in his mouth. 'This is a superhero thing. We'll be back after we kick SixSix's can.'

Something suddenly occurred to him. Reaching into his pocket, Ben pulled out another piece of chocolate. He held it up to Ultimos. 'Hey, want some?'

'Ah, local cuisine.' Ultimos smiled. 'I certainly wouldn't want to offend your planet's customs.'

He took the chocolate, examined it, then popped it in his mouth. He was still chewing when the flickering light of the transporter engulfed them, whisking them off to Earth.

Barely breaking a sweat, Vulkanus poured several tons of iron ore into the back of a flatbed dump truck. Above him hovered SixSix. The bounty hunter held up the canister of Element X and chittered in his strange alien language.

'Once the ore has been purified it can be fused with Element X,' said Vulkanus, his dinosaur-like head pulling into a wicked grin. 'And then – **BOOM!** – the galaxy will be at our feet!'

From behind a nearby tin hut, Ben watched on. 'Now we've got them,' he whispered, turning to the others. 'We'll catch them completely off . . . Ultimos?'

The Galactic Enforcers turned to look at their leader. His bulging, muscular frame was gone. Instead, he stood scrawny and shivering, his blue skin now a deathly shade of grey.

'C-cold,' he trembled. 'So *c-cold.*'

Synaptak hurriedly floated forwards, just in time to catch the falling superhero in his tentacles.

'What's wrong with him?' gasped Ben.

'It appears to be suctratactinite

poisoning,' Synaptak replied. 'But how?' The alien's digital face squinted as he studied Ultimos' mouth. A thin smear of chocolate was just visible on his shrunken lips. 'What is this?' the floating brain demanded.

'I just gave him a little,' said Ben. 'I was just trying to be polite.'

'You did this?' snapped Synaptak. 'I suspected you could not be trusted.'

'Come on,' scoffed Ben. '*Chocolate* is his super-weakness? You have to admit, that's pretty lame!'

'Don't worry, Tini, I have this situation under control,' said Synaptak. He set Ultimos down on the ground and spun towards Ben. 'You'll be dealt with after these rogues are behind bars.'

Before Ben could stop him, the alien brain floated out from behind the hut, and right into the villains' line of sight. 'Galactic Enforcers,' he boomed. 'Engage!'

'What did you do that for?' hissed Ben, as Vulkanus and SixSix readied themselves for combat.

Synaptak scowled. 'As leader, I announced our presence with authority.'

'And let the bad guys know we're here!' added Ben.

The brain's digital face blinked slowly. 'What's your point?'

The two of them were too busy arguing to notice the large shadow passing over them. Luckily, Tini had been paying more attention. She stepped in front, catching a tumbling dump truck before it could crush them.

Synaptak lifted the heavy vehicle with his psychic abilities and launched it back in the direction from which it had come. Vulkanus and SixSix split up to avoid being splattered. The bounty hunter launched himself skyward, while Vulkanus simply dived out of the truck's path.

'By provisions set forth in The Galactic

Code of Conduct, I order you to surrender,' yelled Synaptak. In response, a rain of laser fire tore up the ground around him.

'OK, does that *ever* work?!' demanded Ben as they fled for cover, Tini carrying the shaking Ultimos over one arm.

'Are you finally going to become a Tetrimand?' asked Tini, setting Ultimos safely down behind a rock.

'Not if I can help it,' replied Ben, twirling the dial of the Omnitrix. They already had brute strength on the team. What they needed was

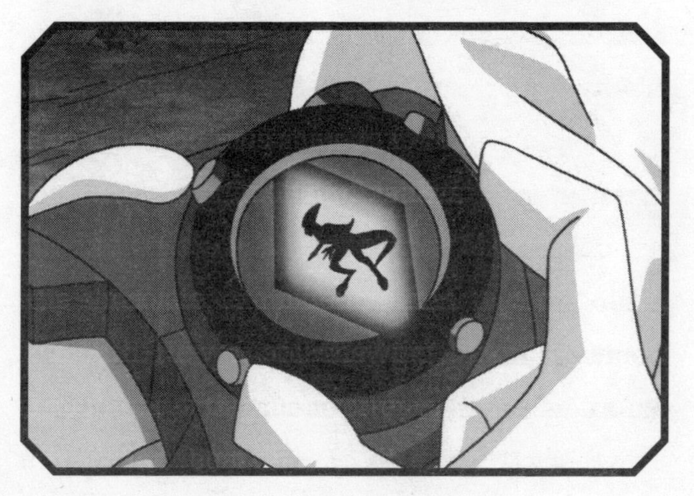

someone a little quicker on their feet.

A cloud of swirling green engulfed him as he activated the watch. In just a few seconds, Ben became the ultra-fast XLR8!

'We've got to split up,' the speedy alien instructed. 'I'll draw their attention and you take out Vulkanus.'

Tini opened her mouth to respond, but a cloud of dust was all that remained where the speedster had stood.

XLR8 rocketed across the quarry floor, dodging SixSix's gunfire easily. Reaching the area directly below the flying bounty hunter, XLR8 began to run in circles. Faster and faster he ran until he was little more than a spinning blur of speed.

SixSix garbled angrily in his alien tongue as XLR8 sent a tornado of sand soaring upwards. The villain was bounced violently around inside the whirlwind before he was eventually thrown free. He hit the ground with a

CRUNCH and lay still, his head left whirling like a washing machine spin-cycle.

Job done, XLR8 shot off, searching for the other alien menace. A huge chunk of machinery slammed down in front of him, blocking his path. Unable to stop in time, the superhero thudded against the metal and tumbled, winded and dazed, to the ground.

Vulkanus roared in triumph and heaved the machinery above his head. XLR8 looked up, only to see the huge hunk of metal come crashing down towards him!

A split second before XLR8 was turned into an alien pancake, Tini slammed a four-fisted punch into Vulkanus, sending him spiralling away. The machinery bounced over the rough ground and came to a rest several metres away.

'What are you doing?' XLR8 demanded, leaping back to his feet. 'You should be dealing with SixSix!'

'No, I must protect you!' Tini replied.

Recovering quickly, Vulkanus grabbed his chunk of machinery again, this time bringing it crashing down on Tini's head. The impact didn't hurt her, but the thick metal pinned her arms to her sides, making it impossible for her to struggle free.

'Tini!' shrieked Synaptak, rushing over. He hit Vulkanus with a powerful psychic blast, driving the monstrous alien back.

But Vulkanus wasn't the only one to be back in action. A miniature transmitter dish emerged from the arm of SixSix's armour and began sending out a high-frequency pulse. As soon as the beam hit Synaptak, the floating brain dropped like a stone. He was unconscious before he hit the ground.

XLR8 rose up on to the balls of his feet, ready for action. The Galactic Enforcers were down. He was the only one left. This was going to be tough!

* * *

'They're getting creamed!' cried Gwen, watching events unfold on the space station's video screen. 'We gotta do something!'

Grandpa's fingers glided across the buttons of the station's control panel. 'Already on it,' he nodded. 'I'm programming in the coordinates. We should be beamed right down into the pit.'

Gwen gulped. 'Should?'

Max punched the final button and, before Gwen could object, they were both swallowed by a twinkling haze of light.

XLR8 moved faster than even he had ever moved before. Laser fire erupted all around him as Vulkanus wildly lobbed rocks and boulders in his direction. They fell like deadly hailstones, shattering the ground on impact.

Avoiding them wasn't proving too difficult, but the Omnitrix was bound to time out on him before long. If XLR8 didn't take these two jokers down soon, he'd be a sitting duck!

SixSix was the biggest threat, so he needed to be taken care of first. At the moment, he was floating well out of XLR8's reach. Still, that wouldn't prove too much of a problem . . .

Gritting his teeth, XLR8 ran faster still. He zig-zagged past falling stones, then made for the quarry wall. Not slowing, he ran straight up the rocky surface, until he was level with the bounty hunter.

Tensing his legs, he sprang backwards and flipped in the air. His feet quickly kicked out – ***BANG! BANG! BANG!*** – against SixSix's jaw, and the villain fell back down to Earth once more.

As XLR8 landed, a shimmering blue haze appeared before him. Grandpa and Gwen stepped from the light, both quietly delighted to have arrived in one piece. Whether they could stay that way, though, was a different matter.

Thanks to Vulkanus, a huge chunk of rock was plunging towards them. XLR8 launched himself forwards, knocking his family out of harm's way just before the boulder hit. He lay on top of them, keeping them covered until he was sure the immediate danger had passed.

'Why didn't we stay in that nice, safe spaceship?' Gwen muttered. She looked up as

XLR8 was lit by a bright-red flash.

Ben stared down at his oversized Galactic Enforcers uniform and groaned. Why did this always happen at the worst possible time? He turned to face the villains, but they were already halfway to their ship.

Vulkanus tore the back of the loaded dump truck away from the rest of the vehicle and hauled it on board. They had what they'd come for. The battle, for them, was over. Well, *almost* over . . .

As the ship took off, it unleashed a barrage of laser fire against the high quarry walls. At once, the stones split and began to tumble down the rock face. Within seconds, they had formed a full-scale landslide, dragging more and more boulders down with them as they hurtled towards the helpless superheroes below!

THROWING AWAY THE RULE BOOK

Ben glanced down at the fallen Galactic Enforcers and realised there was only one thing to do. Racing forward, he stood before the tumbling mass of rocks, his hands on his hips.

'This is a job for Ultra Ben!' he cried. 'Only I can save Tini!'

On hearing Ben's words, Synaptak summoned up reserves of strength he didn't even know he had. If anyone was going to protect Tini, it would be him!

'Step to one side, Earthling,' he instructed. A psychic shockwave radiated from him, meeting the oncoming landslide. As the two collided, the rocks were reduced to a harmless pile of pebbles and sand.

Drained, Synaptak sunk back down to the ground. From inside her metal prison, Tini gave him a grateful smile.

'You can annoy anyone into action,' whispered Gwen to her cousin.

'It's a gift,' Ben replied.

'We've lost SixSix and Vulkanus,' fretted Grandpa Max.

'The bisynthium alloy and Element X can only be bound together with an enormous amount of heat,' wheezed Synaptak.

'Like the forge of a steel mill?' suggested Max, dreading the answer.

'Are there any such facilities in this area?' asked Synaptak.

'*Hello!*' cried Gwen. 'We're in Pittsburgh! Steel town USA!'

Ultimos staggered from behind a rock. He looked almost back to normal, but he was limping as he joined the rest of the team.

'Interesting theory,' he croaked, 'but according to protocol in The Galactic Code of –'

'Forget protocol,' Ben snapped. 'This time we do it the *Tennyson way*!'

In the fiery heart of the closest steel mill, Vulkanus was hard at work. His hands were plunged into a deep container of molten metal as he busily prepared the stolen iron ore.

The hulking monster sighed as SixSix began to chatter excitedly. 'Don't blow a gasket, partner,' he warned. 'Only the purest mixture will combine with Element X to give us the explosive we want!'

The glass canister of Element X clutched tightly in his grip, SixSix nodded. Any minute now it would be ready and they would have everything they needed to rule the galaxy!

Vulkanus took his hands from the melting pot. The liquid metal covering them glowed white hot. He barely felt it.

'Perfect!' He smiled. Nothing could stop them now!

A grinding of metal from above made the villains look up. Synaptak floated down through a hole in the roof, Tini and Ultimos by his side. SixSix took aim with his arm blaster. This would be like shooting fish in a barrel.

Vulkanus sneered. 'You Capes never learn!'

'Wrong!' boomed a voice from behind. A huge, spinning ball spun up from the shadows of the steel plant. It rotated in the air, before slamming into SixSix, sending the bounty hunter sprawling.

'Galactic Enforcers Formation: Surprise Party!' cried Cannonbolt, the largest of Ben's aliens.

'Galactic Enforcers, engage!' yelled Ultimos, and all four superheroes swung into action.

Up in the control room of the steel plant, Gwen and Grandpa pulled levers and fiddled with switches.

'Making steel's like baking a cake,' said Gwen. 'Mess up the recipe and Element X won't bond to it.'

Grandpa nodded. Through the window

above the controls he could see SixSix unleashing a stream of firepower in Cannonbolt's direction. He yanked another lever. They had to act fast.

Lasers, missiles and cluster bombs screeched towards Cannonbolt as SixSix attacked with everything he had. The spinning alien ball bounced and rolled, only just managing to avoid the explosives.

Cannonbolt propelled himself towards the bounty hunter. His fire power used up, SixSix lashed out with a laser whip. It caught Cannonbolt by surprise, sending him tumbling towards a vat of molten iron ore.

Just before the superhero sank down into the glowing hot liquid metal, a bubble of psychic energy wrapped round him. Synaptak gave him a brief nod as he set him safely down on the floor. Cannonbolt nodded back. Maybe Synaptak wasn't *too* much of a jerk after all . . .

Up above them, Ultimos and Tini darted along a metal walkway. Ultimos grinned broadly as they ran. 'This is exhilarating, isn't it?' He beamed. 'No plans! No rules! No –'

Tini slammed her shoulder against him, and both superheroes crunched into the wall. A flaming blob of molten metal tore past them, destroying the walkway.

KA-BOOM! The metal punched a hole straight through the control-room window. Gwen and Grandpa leaped back from the scorching console. They looked down at the ruined control panel. There was no way of messing with the mixture now!

Back out among the furnaces, Vulkanus popped the top off the canister containing the glowing Element X. He held it out, dangling it above the purified iron ore, which swirled in the mixing pot below.

A ground-slam from Tini caused the

whole building to shake. At once, the Element X tumbled from Vulkanus's grip.

Spinning fast, Cannonbolt launched himself towards the falling canister. Catching it just before it broke the surface of the liquid metal, his fingers began to sizzle.

'Hothothothothot!' He grimaced, bouncing the canister from one hand to the other. He didn't have time to tend to his wounds though. Vulkanus and SixSix were already closing in on him, determined to get their explosive back.

Unnoticed by the villains, a large pot of

molten-hot metal floated above their heads. Synaptak lowered it and gave it a quick psychic nudge.

A waterfall of blisteringly hot liquid crashed over them, stopping them in their tracks. Ultimos quickly blasted the molten iron ore with a lungful of ice-cold super-breath. Immediately, the metal hardened, trapping Vulkanus and SixSix.

Cannonbolt rolled up and stood by The Galactic Enforcers, admiring the makeshift prison holding the villains in place. 'I don't know if it's art,' he said, grinning, 'but I like it!'

When Vulkanus and SixSix had been safely beamed to a holding chamber on The Enforcers' space station, Ben shuffled up to Tini.

'Uh . . . about that Tetramand thing.' He winced.

'I have found a new partner,' said Tini, smiling. Synaptak floated up behind her and rested a tentacle on her shoulder.

'Ben, your unorthodox methods are exactly what we need to tackle this new breed of criminal,' said Ultimos, handing Ben a badge. 'We officially extend to you a full commission in The Galactic Enforcers.'

Ben glanced at it, then back at his grandpa and cousin. 'Thanks,' he said, 'but no, thanks. I'm already part of a super-team.'

'Keep it,' said Ultimos with a smile, 'in the hope that we meet again someday.' A blue light surrounded the three superheroes. 'Galactic Enforcers, away!' And with that they were gone.

Gwen stepped closer to her cousin. 'You really mean all that stuff you said to Ultimos about already being part of a super-team?' she asked.

Ben turned to face her. 'Nah!' he said, breaking into a grin. 'But who wants to hang with a pack of wackos like that? I'm better off with you guys!'

Ben 10 Alien Force Annual 2010	978 1 4052 4653 8; £7.99
Ben 10 Alien Force colour storybook 1 (Ben 10 Returns Part 1/Part 2)	978 1 4052 4799 3; £4.99
Ben 10 Alien Force colour storybook 2 (The Gauntlet/Be-Knighted)	978 1 4052 4800 6; £4.99
Ben 10 Amazing 3D Hero Vision	978 1 4052 4413 8; £3.99
Ben 10 Puzzle and Quiz Book	978 1 4052 4492 3; £3.99
Ben 10 Magnet Book	978 1 4052 4599 9; £5.99
Ben 10 All Action Stories & Flicker Book	978 1 4052 4512 8; £4.99
Ben 10 comic book 1 (And Then There Were 10)	978 1 4052 4663 7; £4.99
Ben 10 comic book 2 (Washington B.C.)	978 1 4052 4664 4; £4.99
Ben 10 comic book 3 (The Krakken)	978 1 4052 4804 4; £4.99

Ben 10 comic book 4 (Permanent Retirement)	978 1 4052 4805 1; £4.99
Ben 10 chapter storybook 1 (And Then There Were 10/Kevin 11)	978 1 4052 4467 1; £3.99
Ben 10 chapter storybook 2 (The Alliance/Secrets)	978 1 4052 4468 8; £3.99
Ben 10 chapter storybook 3 (Truth/Framed)	978 1 4052 4672 9; £4.99
Ben 10 chapter storybook 4 (The Galactic Enforcers/Ultimate Weapon)	978 1 4052 4673 6; £4.99

COMING SOON . . .

3 COOL NEW BEN 10 BOOKS!

Ben 10 Alien Force Extreme (Pop-Up)	978 1 4052 4852 5; £14.99
Ben 10 Alien Force chapter storybook 1 (All That Glitters/Max Out)	978 1 4052 5006 1; £4.99
Ben 10 Alien Force chapter storybook 2 (Paradox/Plumbers' Helpers)	978 1 4052 5007 8; £4.99

Visit Egmont.co.uk